Born Under a Star

Written by Erwin Buchholz
Illustrated by Barbara Legg

PublishAmerica
Baltimore

First printing

ISBN: 978-1-61546-130-1
PUBLISHED BY PUBLISHAMERICA, LLLP
www.publishamerica.com
Baltimore

Printed in the United States of America

To Coral, with all my love.

Mildred was a mottled chicken. She lived in a large hen house.

She was different from the other hens. Her feet were big and her toes stuck out. She had wobbly legs and knobby knees. Her feathers were drab and thinned out in places. All the other chickens had small feet, slim legs and sleek, shiny feathers.

Everyone teased Mildred about the way she looked. They would say, "Mildred, why don't you comb your feathers?" or "Mildred, why don't you walk straight?"
But Mildred paid no attention to them. She remembered what her mother told her, and she would tell the others.

"I was born under a star. That's why I am the way I am."
The other chickens would laugh.
"Ha-ha! Ha-ha!" they cackled.
Then Mildred would look at her wobbly legs and tattered feathers. She wished she could be like the others, but she could only sigh.

One evening it was Mildred's turn to gather the eggs. She picked them up one at a time and cradled them in her wing. Doris saw her and shrieked, "Mildred, you're doing it all wrong!"

You're supposed to gather the eggs in the basket."
Mildred set the eggs down and took the basket from the shelf. Then she laid the eggs gently in the basket.

Then Dorella shouted, "Mildred, you're doing it wrong. Put some straw in the basket first or you'll break the eggs."
Mildred emptied the basket one egg at a time. Then she found some straw and put the eggs back while the others glared at her.
"Don't drop the eggs, set them down gently," cried one chicken.
"Don't drag the basket, lift it," crowed another. One by one they all had something to say about what Mildred was doing wrong.

At last she was finished. She picked up the basket full of eggs and started for the door, but a nail caught her big toe. Mildred tumbled forward and landed splat on top of the eggs.
"Oh Mildred, you're so clumsy," scolded Doris.
"Yes, Mildred's done it again," squawked Dorella.

"Ha-ha! Ha-ha! They all cackled while Mildred began to wipe the egg off her face. The more she wiped, the messier she got. Harriet, a plump hen, waddled forward.
"Mildred, you're doing it all wrong!"
She pulled Mildred's kerchief from her hand. Harriet pulled so hard that Mildred fell once again in the puddle of broken eggs, and the cackling began once more.
"Ha-ha! Ha-ha!" But Mildred didn't care.

She ran into the cold, dark night, through the tall grass and toward the stable. Finding an old milk stool, she perched on the handle and began to sulk.

"You're doing it wrong! You're doing it wrong! That's all they ever say."

"I know just how you feel, I do," a gruff voice brayed.
"Wh-who's there?" cried Mildred, alarmed. She turned and saw the biggest donkey ever.

"I'm Fred, I am. F-R-E-D, Fred," said the donkey.
"Not Frederick or Freddie, just plain Fred."
"Well how do you do, Just-Plain-Fred?"

The donkey trundled forward and stood in the doorway.
"Left-Feet-Fred, that's what they call me. But you can call me Fred."
The donkey looked out at the sky where a star blazed brightly.
"I was born under a star just like that one yonder," said Fred.

"I was born under a star, too," said Mildred. "At least that's what my mother told me."
"Then you are a princess."
"Who, Me?"
"Yes sir. Sure as my name's Fred, and you can bet it is. Anyone born under a star is nothing less."
Mildred looked at her big feet. She looked at her wobbly knees and tattered feathers matted with dried egg yolk. Then she looked at the donkey, grey and old with deep, tired eyes.

"I don't feel like a princess and besides, we don't live in a castle," she said.
That doesn't make no never mind," said Fred, his eyes fixed on the star. It seemed to have grown brighter and was almost above their heads.

Suddenly there was a commotion. Two people scurried into the stable from the far end. Feet shuffled quickly about and to Mildred's surprise a newborn baby began to cry.

The star blazed ever so brightly. Mildred thought it would burst. The field outside began to glow and the stillness was broken with the chorus of a thousand angels.

Sounds of merriment and laughter grew louder and louder until at once a voice called out, "Over here! We found him!"
Soon the stable was full of excited people singing and laughing about the good news of a newborn king.

Mildred's heart was beating wildly. "I must tell the others", she said. She fluttered back to the hen house cackling loudly, waking the others in fright.
"Come quick, come quick! A king has been born and I've seen his star," was all she could say.
"Oh Mildred, you and your star," said the others, but they saw that Mildred would not be silenced until they followed her to the barn.

One by one they marched into the stable and saw nothing but a tiny baby wrapped in old cloths cradled by a peasant woman. There were no shepherds or angels, only two weary travelers and a small child. Except for the star, the sky was as dark as ever.

"It's just another baby," Doris scowled. One by one they left the stable, hissing at Mildred as they walked by.

Mildred and Fred stood silently watching the babe. Instead of pyjamas, he was wrapped in dirty old rags. The smell of camels filled the air, and there was no water to wash the tiny creature's face.

"Is he really a king?" whispered Mildred.
"A very special one," replied Fred.
Mildred looked closely at Fred's shaggy mane and long, thick ears. She looked at his wrinkled brow and deep brown eyes. He looked very wise and peaceful.

Mildred looked once more at the blazing star high above the stable. She remembered the shepherds' laughter and the angels' songs.
Feeling very special for the first time in her life, Mildred breathed a deep, contented sigh. At last she understood what it meant to be born under a star.

LaVergne, TN USA
04 November 2009
162940LV00003B